STILL HOLDING THE POSTCARD, Rosemary Rita turned the hourglass over. As the sand in the glass began to drip down to the bottom, she felt funny, kind of light in the head. Her stomach felt queasy, as if she'd just stepped off a roller-coaster ride. Suddenly everything became blurry. She tried to sit down on the bed, but fell back into the pillows. Before she knew it, she had fallen into a deep, deep sleep.

When Rosemary Rita awoke, she realized that she was not in her bed, or even her room. Still a little groggy from being asleep, she slowly looked around and wondered, "Where am I? How'd I get out of my room? I must be dreaming!"

BY BARBARA ROBERTSON

Hourglass Adventures

№ 1

ROSEMARY
MEETS
ROSEMARIE

WINSLOW PRESS

FLORIDA NEW YORK

Library of Congress Cataloging-in-Publication Data
Robertson, Barbara
Rosemary Meets Rosemarie / by Barbara Robertson.—1ˢᵗ ed.
p. cm.— (The hourglass adventures; #1)
Summary: For her tenth birthday, Rosemary Rita's grandmother
Mimi sends her a magical hourglass, which takes Rosemary Rita
back to 1870 in Germany to meet Mimi's great-grandmother
and help her decode a mysterious postcard.
ISBN: 1-890817-55-4
[1. Great-grandmothers—Fiction. 2. Grandmothers—Fiction.
3. Magic—Fiction. 4. Time travel—Fiction. 5. Ciphers—Fiction.
6. Germany—History—1848–1870—Fiction.] I. Title.

PZ7.R54466 Ro 2001
00-043407   [Fic]—dc21

Creative Director
Bretton Clark

Editor
Margery Cuyler

Designer
Annemarie Cofer

PRINTED IN THE UNITED STATES OF AMERICA
First edition, 05/01

WINSLOW PRESS

**Discover *The Hourglass Adventures*' interactive Web site with
worldwide links, games, activities, and more at winslowpress.com**

HOME OFFICE   ALL INQUIRIES
770 East Atlantic Avenue, Suite 201   115 East 23ʳᵈ Street, 10ᵗʰ Floor
Delray Beach, FL 33483   New York, NY 10010

To the memory of **my Grandmother,**

Rosemary,

whose **generous** heart and **adventurous** spirit

inspired this book.

Chapter I
MEET·ROSEMARY·RITA

ROSEMARY RITA INHERITED her brown hair from her dad, her rosy cheeks from her mom, and her name and love of postcards from her grandmother, Rosemary Regina. As far back as Rosemary Rita could remember, she and Mimi, as she called her grandmother, had exchanged postcards. Rosemary Rita saved all of them in a big box under her bed. She kept them organized by year.

The early ones that she sent to her grand-

Postcard sent to Mimi by Rosemary Rita, age 4

mother in New York were filled with scribbles and letters and pictures.

Rosemary Rita couldn't wait to hear back from Mimi. When she was expecting a postcard, she would run to meet the mailman. Mimi's early postcards were written in large letters with pictures for some of the words. Rosemary Rita had refused to let her mother read those postcards, insisting that they were *her* mail and that *she* could read them all by herself.

Postcard from Mimi, received by Rosemary Rita, age 5

Over the years, Rosemary Rita still got excited when the postcards came. She would answer them right away, sending a postcard back to Mimi about whatever popped into her head. Sometimes she would practice her poetry. Other times she would write about what she was doing in school. When something important happened to

Rosemary Rita, she immediately got in touch with her grandmother. For example, in third grade, Rosemary Rita won the lead in the school play. The very first thing she did was dash off a postcard.

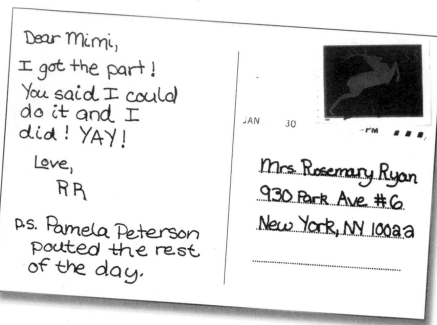

Dear Mimi,
I got the part!
You said I could do it and I did! YAY!
Love,
RR
p.s. Pamela Peterson pouted the rest of the day.

JAN 30 —PM

Mrs. Rosemary Ryan
930 Park Ave. #6
New York, NY 10022

Postcard sent to Mimi by Rosemary Rita, age 8

Their latest thing was to send each other messages in secret codes. Rosemary Rita felt like a detective decoding the messages.

Sometimes they'd send each other a riddle

to decipher. Even better than breaking the code, the fun part for Rosemary Rita was seeing the puzzled look on her mother's face as she handed over the postcard.

Super Secrets:

Send a coded message
at winslowpress.com

Rosemary Rita became such a pro, it only took her twenty minutes to crack the code below.

Dear Rosemary Rita,
Remember that sometimes the best place to begin is at the end. That advice should be good for a chuckle.

Z XLDYLB ILWV GL ZM RMM LM UIRWZB, SV HGZBVW GDL MRTSGH, GSVM OVUG LM UIRWZB. SLD XZM GSZG YV? ZMHDVI: SRH SLIHV DZH MZNVW UIRWZB.

Love,
Mimi

Miss R.R. Hampton
465 Hillside St.
Greenville, SC 29604

Postcard from Mimi, received by Rosemary Rita, age 9

Using the clue from Mimi—to start at the end—she quickly figured out that each letter stood for another letter. This is the chart that she made:

a	b	c	d	e	f	g	h	i	j	k	l	m	n	o	p	q	r	s	t	u	v	w	x	y	z
z	y	x	w	v	u	t	s	r	q	p	o	n	m	l	k	j	i	h	g	f	e	d	c	b	a

Then Rosemary Rita plugged in the right letters to discover this riddle:

Z XLDYLB ILWV GL ZM RMM LM
a cowboy rode to an inn on

UIRWZB, SV HGZBVW GDL MRTSGH,
friday, he stayed two nights,

GSVM OVUG LM UIRWZB.
then left on friday.

SLD XZM GSZG YV?
how can that be?

ZMHDVI: SRH SLIHV DZH MZNVW UIRWZB.
answer: his horse was named friday.

For the answer to this riddle, see page 19.

Of course, Mimi sent Rosemary Rita post-cards on every special occasion. Birthdays,

Christmas, Easter, even Groundhog Day.

But on Rosemary Rita's tenth birthday, her grandmother did *not* send a postcard! Rosemary Rita was sitting on her front stoop waiting for Mr. Leonard, the mailman, to arrive. It was a warm spring day. The bright pink azalea bushes and the dogwood tree in the front yard were in full bloom. Rosemary Rita thought about how springtime arrived in her hometown of Greenville, South Carolina, almost a full month before it visited her grandmother in New York.

"Hey there, Rosemary Rita," said Mr. Leonard as he walked up the brick path toward her.

"Oh, hi, Mr. Leonard," she answered, tapping her foot impatiently. "Have anything for me?"

"You know I do. Now, let me see here."

He picked a few pieces from his pile and handed them over.

"Thank you, thank you, Mr. Leonard," she said, grabbing the letters and darting inside. She ran up the stairs, down the hall, and into her bedroom, shutting the door behind her. Kicking off her clogs, she flung her stuffed animals between the bedposts and flopped across her bed. She carefully arranged the cards in front of her like an open fan.

There were two cards from her cousins, Sarah and Amy—always fun to read. There was an invitation to Lisa's birthday party—should be a good time. Finally, there was a notice from the post office. But where was the postcard from Mimi?

Ridiculous Riddles:

Decode the answers to goofy gigglers at winslowpress.com

Rosemary Rita stared at the notice again. It said that there were packages being held for her at the post office. She jumped up from her bed, nearly tripping on the pile of books on the floor, and raced downstairs to find her mother.

"Hey, Mom, look at this. What does it mean? Will you take me to the post office? Now, will you, please?" Rosemary Rita pleaded.

"Okay, okay, honey. Just as soon as I finish feeding your brother."

Rosemary Rita mumbled under her breath, "We'll probably be here until my ELEVENTH birthday."

She watched as her two-year-old brother, Ryan, threw his plastic sippy cup to the floor, not once, not twice, but SIX times. Her mother never complained, just stooped to pick it up again and again!

Rosemary Rita thought about how peaceful her life had been before her brother was born two years ago. Until then, she had had her mother and father all to herself. Now, Mom and Dad were always too busy taking care of Ryan to do things with her, or so it seemed. Mom said that Ryan was a "handful" and that she couldn't leave him alone for a second. Rosemary Rita had to admit that much was true. Only last week, the little troublemaker drew with permanent marker all over the new rug in the living room. Her mother was furious with him for about a minute, two minutes, tops. When Ryan said, "Don't cry, Mama, I draw picture for you. I sorry, Mama, I fix it," Mom just picked him up and hugged him.

"Boy, I never would have gotten off so easy," thought Rosemary Rita.

That same night, Rosemary Rita had written Mimi all about the rug incident.

Dear Mimi,
You'll never believe what happened. Ryan ruined the new rug, and he only had to sit in time-out for 2 minutes! I would've been grounded for the rest of my life.
It's just not fair!!!
Write back soon.
    Love,
        RR

Mrs. Rosemary Ryan
930 Park Ave. #6
New York, NY 10022

Mimi wrote back some words of advice:

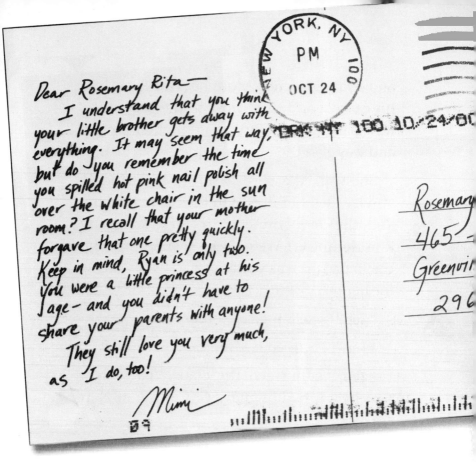

Dear Rosemary Rita—

I understand that you think your little brother gets away with everything. It may seem that way, but do you remember the time you spilled hot pink nail polish all over the white chair in the sun room? I recall that your mother forgave that one pretty quickly. Keep in mind, Ryan is only two. You were a little princess at his age—and you didn't have to share your parents with anyone! They still love you very much, as I do, too!

Mimi

Rosemary
465-
Greenvil
296

Even today, on her birthday, Rosemary Rita didn't feel like a princess. Ryan always came first, and it was taking *forever* for Mom to finish feeding him. "I'm going to wait in the car!" Rosemary Rita shouted as she marched out to the driveway and climbed into the Suburban.

Finally, after what seemed like hours, Mom

and Ryan appeared. Mom buckled Ryan into his car seat and they drove to the post office. Rosemary Rita couldn't wait another second and was glad there was no line.

She walked anxiously up to the window and handed her notice to the clerk. Looking at it, the clerk grinned. "So you're Rosemary Rita Hampton? We've been wondering who the lucky girl was with ten packages waiting for her."

"Ten?" exclaimed Rosemary Rita.

"Ten?!" echoed her mother.

"Ten," confirmed the clerk. "They were sent by a Mrs. Rosemary G. Carlisle in New York."

"That's my grandmother Mimi!" shouted Rosemary Rita. "She didn't forget!"

The clerk's eyes crinkled with pleasure as she pushed package after package across the counter. She even helped Rosemary Rita and her mom make two trips back and forth to the car with all of the boxes.

As they drove home, Rosemary Rita's head was in a whirl. What was inside the boxes?

She was so deep in thought, she didn't even flinch when Ryan pulled her hair.

Finally they turned onto Creekside Drive and were home at last. Bounding out of the car before it fully stopped, Rosemary Rita raced into the house, carrying as many boxes as she could manage.

"Rosemary Rita Hampton, you come back here. You could've killed yourself jumping out of the car like that," her mother yelled.

But Rosemary Rita didn't hear a word. She was already climbing the stairs to her bedroom, two at a time.

Answer to riddle on page 12: HIS HORSE WAS NAMED FRIDAY.

Chapter 2

THE·TEN·BOXES

W HEN ROSEMARY RITA
had finally dragged all
of the boxes up the
stairs and into her room, she col-
lapsed on the rug. As she caught
her breath, she noticed there was
a number on each box. In no
time, she had lined them up
from one to ten against the wall.
Using her scissors to cut the tape on
the first box, she pulled the cardboard
flaps apart. Inside was a bundle wrapped in
yellowed tissue paper with a handwritten
note from her grandmother taped to it. The
note read:

To Rosemary

from the desk of
~ Rosemary Regina ~

Happy Birthday to my darling little Rosemary!

A few months ago, when I was cleaning out your great-grandmother's attic, I came across these boxes. I was so delighted to find this long-lost treasure that I hadn't seen in more than fifty years. I decided right then and there that I would wait until your tenth birthday to share it with you. I knew that you, more than anyone else, would appreciate the contents.

Inside this box are some of the very first postcards ever sent. They were collected by your

-1-   (over)

·22·

Happy Birthday to my darling little Rosemary! A few months ago, when I was cleaning out your great-grandmother's attic, I came across these boxes. I was so delighted to find this long-lost treasure that I hadn't seen in more than fifty years. I decided right then that I would wait until your tenth birthday to share it with you. I knew that you, more than anyone else, would appreciate the contents.

Inside this box are some of the very first postcards ever sent. They were collected by your great-great-great-grandmother, Rosemary Ruth Berger Christianson. She was the first Rosemary in our family and our first collector of postcards. Remember that old photograph on the chest in the foyer that you always thought was so beautiful? Well, that is the Rosemary I'm talking about. Anyway, as you have probably already figured out, some of these postcards are well over a hundred years old! Rosemary Ruth wasn't the only one to save postcards and special memorabilia. Her daughter and the other Rosemarys who followed all contributed. Sweetie, I hope that you will experience the "magic" of the postcards. I trust you to take good care of our treasure. Again, happy birthday!

With love,

Grandma Mimi

P.S. The other boxes contain items that the Rosemarys have saved. Remember, what at first may appear to be a worthless piece of paper or a broken item was once very dear to a young Rosemary. You will understand what I mean soon enough. Enjoy these happy memories, for they now belong to you.

P.P.S. In Box #10 is an object wrapped in shiny red paper with a gold bow. Promise you'll wait until I talk with you before opening that one!

Rosemary Rita's heart pounded as she looked at the packages that lined the wall. What did all of this mean? "I guess I'd better open the next one," she said to herself. She then tore into Box #2 and pulled out a cloth bundle.

Birthday Bash:

Design your own birthday cards, invitations, and more at winslowpress.com

"Cool!" said Rosemary Rita as she unwrapped it. "Look at this dress! I wonder if my great-great-great-grandmother Rosemary Ruth wore this when she was my age!"

The long dress was dark gray. It had lace around the collar and buttons going down the front.

Rosemary Rita yanked off her blue jeans and long-sleeved T-shirt and slipped into the antique dress. The sleeves were a little short, and she couldn't fasten the top button. Still, she felt special in the dress as she swirled through the room with the skirt billowing out around her.

Looking in the box again, she found a creamy white pinafore and a beautiful woolen cape. She slipped the pinafore over her head and whirled around again. Then she reached for the cloak and threw it over her shoulders. As she looked at herself in the full-length mirror that hung on her closet door, her breath caught in her throat. She looked like one of the figurines on the shelf in the study downstairs.

Rosemary Rita never spent much time fussing in front of the mirror. It embarrassed her when people said things like: "You have the prettiest green eyes I've ever seen!" or "I would give anything to be as tall and thin as you." Even now, she looked right past her own reflection and tried to imagine how a certain Rosemary might have looked wearing the same cloak.

Time Capsule:

What would you save in your special box?
Visit winslowpress.com

She picked up the bundle with the old postcards in them and noticed that they looked different from the ones she was used to. The writing was on the front under the pictures, and there were even some without any pictures at all.

As she flipped through the postcards, she started putting them in order by date, just the way she did with her own collection. Her fingers trembled as she thought of the other Rosemarys in her family who had touched the very same cards she was touching today.

The oldest postcard lay on top when she waas finished. It was dated September 28, 1870. Yellowed with ragged edges, it had an eagle and a military symbol on the front. There was also an elaborate postage stamp.

Mailmania:
Send an e-card to a friend
at winslowpress.com

Rosemary Rita looked at the card more closely. It was addressed to Fräulein Rosemarie Ruth Berger in Berlin, Germany. The words were written in a fancy, faded script. Still, it was readable—if she could read German, that is!

"I've got to find out what this message says!" thought Rosemary Rita. "But who can help me? Maybe somebody wrote down a translation somewhere." She eagerly examined the boxes again. "I'll bet Mimi was curious, too," she thought. "I can't wait to call her and find out what this is all about."

Rosemary Rita opened Box #3. There she found a glimmering rock, a feather, a newspaper article, a coin, and a broken locket, but still no clue to the message on the postcards. In Box #4, there was just more clothing. A beautiful red scarf stood out against the other drably-colored items. It reminded her of her grandmother's words about the shiny red package in the last box. She picked up the old postcard written in German again. "I'll bet that package will help me solve the mystery," thought Rosemary Rita. "I *have* to open it. I'm sure Mimi would understand if I take just *one* little peek. It wouldn't hurt just to look," she thought as she ripped open Box #10 and pulled out the specially wrapped package. She hesitated for only a second, then tore off the gold bow. Yanking the red paper away, she gasped as an antique hourglass fell into her lap. It was amazing! The stand was made of intricately carved wood. Etched on the ends was a scene showing a person standing near a boat on the water. It had some sort of ancient writing carved on it that she couldn't understand.

Still holding the postcard, Rosemary Rita turned the hourglass over. As the sand in the glass began to drip down to the bottom, she felt funny, kind of light in the head. Her stomach felt queasy, as if she'd just stepped off a roller-coaster ride. Suddenly everything became blurry. She tried to sit down on the bed, but fell back into the pillows. Before she knew it, she had fallen into a deep, deep sleep.

Chapter 3

Back·In·Time

WHEN ROSEMARY RITA awoke, she realized that she was not in her bed, or even in her room. Still a little groggy from being asleep, she slowly looked around and wondered, "Where am I? How'd I get out of my room? I must be dreaming!"

Just then a carriage pulled by two horses came speeding toward her. She jumped out of the way. The dust from the dirt road sprayed into her eyes, making them water.

"Whoa! This is no dream!" Rosemary Rita rubbed her eyes to get the dust out. Her head spinning, she sat down on the grass by the side of the road. Before she had time to figure out whether to yell or cry, a girl about her age came walking over the hill.

Rosemary Rita wanted to run, but something familiar about the girl made her freeze. She had seen her before. But where?

The girl walked right up to her and started talking. It was the strangest thing. Rosemary Rita could tell that the girl was not speaking English, yet she could understand every word.

The girl spoke again. "Are you all right? It looks like you've been crying."

Sprich Deutsch:

Check out the German audio phrasebook at winslowpress.com

"I, uh, well…" Rosemary Rita knew her eyes were red from the dust, but she did not know what to say. If she told the girl that a few minutes ago she had been in her room and now she was standing out here in the country dodging horses, it would sound crazy.

"You look like you're lost. Do you need directions?" the girl asked.

"Yes, I guess I am lost," she managed to say. "I got separated from my parents and little brother. All of my things are with them. I don't have any shoes or money and I have no idea where I am," Rosemary Rita blurted. To her amazement, the girl understood her, too.

"Well, you are on Leipziger Strauss, down the road from Elisabethschool. My name is Rosemarie Ruth Berger, and I live around the corner. I was just on my way home for lunch."

Rosemary Rita's knees buckled, and she sank to the ground. She could not believe her ears. Did this girl really say that she was Rosemarie Ruth Berger? It couldn't be, but as she looked at the girl's eyes, she knew that it was true. She had seen those eyes before in that old photograph at Mimi's house. They were the same color green as her own eyes, and she had the same round, rosy cheeks, too. If Rosemarie's hair were not blond and carefully styled, they would look like twins.

"Oh my gosh, you are my gr..." Rosemary Rita stopped herself. She couldn't tell this ten-year-old that she was a great-great-great-grandmother. Yet she needed to say something. "You are great to come along when you did. I don't know where my parents are, and I need some help finding them. We were on a trip and sometime after breakfast, I hit my head, and I can't really remember much after that. I don't even know where I am or what day it is or why I'm halfway dressed." Rosemary Rita crossed her fingers behind her back and hoped Rosemarie bought her story.

She must have believed her, because Rosemarie reached out and gently helped Rosemary Rita to her feet. "Now, don't worry, I'll help you. *Wie heissen Sie?*

What's your name?" she asked.

"I'm Ro—" Rosemary Rita had to stop herself again. She couldn't say her whole name. "I'm Rita Hampton," she said nervously.

"Well, Rita, you are in Berlin, and today is Tuesday, 5 October. I think that you should come home with me. My mother would be happy to give you something to eat, and we will try to help you find your parents. I can lend you some shoes, too."

"Okay, thanks. I *am* hungry, and my feet are kind of cold. Um, Rosemarie, you say that it's October 5th. In which year?"

"You really did hurt your head. Why, 1870, of course."

Great-great-great-grandmother?

Get to know Rosemarie
at winslowpress.com

"1870, of course," repeated Rosemary Rita, feeling lightheaded again. She took a deep breath and tried to let everything sink in. All she had done was turn over an hourglass, and suddenly she was a hundred and thirty-one years back in time talking to her great-great-great-grandmother in Germany! She really was in trouble now, probably the biggest trouble she had ever been in. Definitely worse than when she snuck out of the house to roller blade with her friend Annie. This time she had not only snuck out of the house, she'd snuck out of the country, not to mention the century!

"Rita, are you all right? Rita, can you hear me?"

"Uh, oh, yes, I'm fine. I am pretty hungry. Maybe I'll feel better when I get something to eat," she murmured.

"Well, come on, then. Let's go to my *Wohnung*, apartment."

Dodging carriages, peddlers, and pedestrians, they walked side by side down the dirt road as they made their way to Rosemarie's.

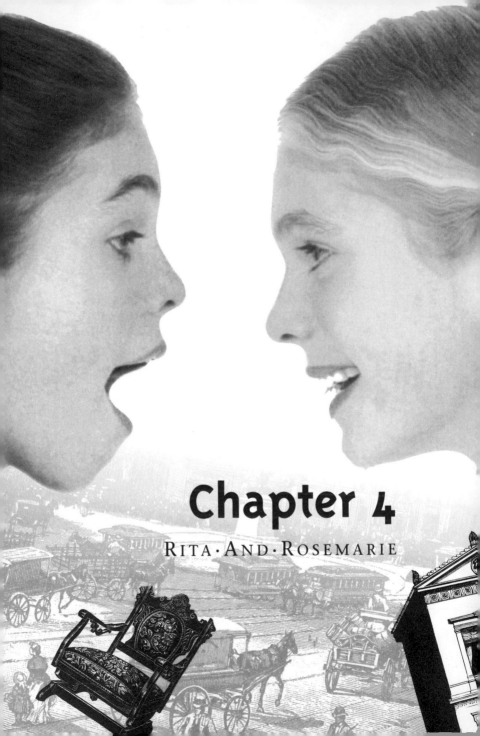

Chapter 4

RITA·AND·ROSEMARIE

IT DID NOT TAKE THE TWO GIRLS long to reach the Bergers' apartment. As they walked, Rosemary Rita thought, "I can't believe I am going to see how my ancestors lived. I'll get to meet them and talk to them and understand them! I wish I could tell Rosemarie that we're related and that I'm from the future, but I'd better not now.

Probably not ever. She'd think I was crazy."

Passing through the courtyard, Rosemarie pointed out the horse stable and her father's workshop behind the building. They opened the front door, climbed a flight of stairs, and headed down a narrow hall to the Bergers' home.

The family lived in an apartment with six rooms. As they walked through the front hallway, Rosemarie paused to hang their cloaks in the large armoire while Rosemary Rita looked around. She noticed a formal sitting room on her left. It had a settee, a tidy little sewing table, two velvet winged chairs, a wooden hutch, and a baby grand piano. On the other side of the hallway was a small but lovely dining room. Rosemarie led her new friend Rita to the heart of the Berger home, the kitchen. Delicious smells came from the large stone fireplace that took up one whole wall. Gleaming copper pots and dried bundles of herbs hung on the opposite wall. There was a large window with a view of the courtyard, and a door that led to an outside set of stairs. In the middle of the room was a long table with ten chairs. Rosemary Rita immediately felt comfortable and welcome in this warm room. She smiled as she watched the happy scene.

A pretty woman with dark blond hair piled on top of her head was seated at the table. She wore a long green woolen dress with a starched white apron and was reading to a young boy. He was dressed in a white collared shirt and wool knickers, long socks, and brown shoes. He snuggled close to the woman, leaning his head on her shoulder.

Costume Shop:

Dress up Rosemary Rita
at winslowpress.com

Rosemarie walked up to the woman and hugged her, then tousled the boy's hair.

"Mother, *dies ist meine Freundin.* This is my friend, Rita Hampton," said Rosemarie. "Could she join us for dinner?"

"Of course, dear. We're just about to start. Tell Lina to set another plate." Frau Berger turned to Rosemary Rita. "*Sehr erfreut.* It is a pleasure to meet you."

"It's very nice to meet you, too," Rosemary Rita replied.

Rosemarie then introduced Rosemary Rita to her younger brother, Fritz.

"You don't have any shoes on!" Fritz said, pointing to Rosemary Rita's bare feet.

"Fritz!" exclaimed Frau Berger.

Rosemary Rita's cheeks turned bright red. "I, uh, lost them," she stammered.

"Don't worry, dear, you can borrow a pair of my daughter's," Frau Berger said. Then she noticed the size of Rosemary Rita's feet. "Or mine," she said quickly. She sent Rosemarie to get a pair out of her armoire. When Rosemarie returned with a pair of brown leather boots, Rosemary Rita put them on and laced them up to her ankles. The boots pinched her toes a bit, but she didn't complain.

A few minutes later, Meister Wilhelm Berger came into the room, followed by three men. Meister Berger was a large, handsome man with a ruddy complexion. His short blond hair was neatly combed, and his moustache was waxed at the corners like two backward Cs. He was fingering his pocket watch while deep in conversation with his companions.

"That's my father with the blond hair. He just hired a new apprentice named Karl," whispered Rosemarie. "He's the man with the dark hair. The man with the glasses is also an apprentice. The younger man is Papa's assistant, Peter. I'll introduce them when they stop talking."

A slender, teenaged girl—clearly Lina—rushed around the room, placing platters of food on the table. She set a place next to Rosemarie for Rosemary Rita.

As Rosemary Rita looked at the blue-and-white china and the delicious-looking plates of food, she couldn't believe they ate lunch like this every day.

"How long do you have to eat?" she asked Rosemarie.

"Two hours," she answered. "Like everyone else."

"If Rosemarie only knew," thought

Rosemary Rita. "I only get thirty minutes to wolf down a boring peanut butter and jelly sandwich."

Everyone at the table was discussing a war. Rosemary Rita tried to figure out which war they were talking about. She wished she knew more about European history, but they studied that in the older grades.

They were also talking a lot about a young man named Martin. Rosemary Rita leaned over and whispered to Rosemarie, "Who's Martin?"

"He's my older brother. He's eighteen years old."

"You have an eighteen-year-old *and* a three-year-old brother?" Rosemary Rita asked.

"Actually, I also had two sisters. They died when they were babies."

"Oh, I'm so sorry." Rosemary Rita felt terrible. She shouldn't have opened her big mouth. She looked over at Rosemarie, who

Marvelous Martin:

All about Martin
at winslowpress.com

was eating her lunch and laughing at something Karl, the apprentice, had said. Rosemary Rita thought about Ryan. He was a pain in the neck, but she couldn't imagine life without him.

Rosemary Rita started paying attention again to what people were saying. It was so interesting. Frau Berger was still talking about Martin.

"I can't help but worry about him, Wilhelm," she remarked to Rosemarie's father. "It is not safe for him to be in France right now."

"Gabi, he will be fine. Theo will take good care of him. Besides, they are not actually fighting in the war, just writing about it. Theo is a well-respected writer. They have papers from our Prussian government stating that they are civilians. Theo promised that they would stay in areas that are controlled by our army."

Her husband's words did not soothe Frau Berger. Her forehead was crisscrossed with worry lines.

The girls finished their lunch, and Lina cleared their plates. Rosemarie pulled Rosemary Rita close to her and said in a low voice, "Do you want me to tell Papa about your parents now?"

Just as she was about to respond, there was a knock at the back door. Frau Berger opened the door and said, "Hello, Sven. Do come in."

The young man entered and quickly removed his cap. He smoothed down his thick, curly hair and said, "Excuse me, Frau and Meister Berger. I did not mean to interrupt your meal, but I have news straight from the palace."

"What is it, Sven? Do tell us," Meister Berger said.

"You have been commissioned by the crown prince to make a light wagon! They would like you to begin working on it immediately."

"Oh, Wilhelm! I'm so proud. What an honor!" Frau Berger said as she ran to hug him.

"Papa, that is wonderful!" Rosemarie cried.

"Hooray for Papa!" said Fritz. The room erupted with laughter and cheering.

Kings and Queens:

Get the scoop on royal families at winslowpress.com

In all the confusion, Rosemarie forgot about asking her father to help find Rita's parents and announced that it was time to get back to school.

"Why don't you come with me? Or would you rather wait here until I get back?" she whispered to Rosemary Rita.

No way was Rosemary Rita going to stay here by herself. Besides, she was interested in seeing what they did in school way back then.

"I'll come with you," she mouthed back.

Their good-byes were barely heard with all of the chatter about the new wagon. The girls put on their cloaks, slipped out, and started the two-mile walk to the Elisabethschool.

As they walked, Rosemarie told Rosemary Rita about her older brother, Martin. "He is my hero. He might be eight years older than I am, but he never treats me like a baby.

I didn't want him to go to France with Uncle Theo. I agree with Mother that it is too dangerous."

Just then, Rosemary Rita thought of the postcard addressed to Fräulein Rosemarie Ruth Berger. She tried to picture it in her mind. Was it from Martin? She wasn't sure, but she was guessing that it was.

Rosemary Rita asked, "Have you heard from Martin since he's been in France?"

Rosemarie nodded. "I've gotten two letters from him. The first letter was mostly about the trip from Berlin to France. The trip took much longer than they had expected. Martin didn't seem to mind. He was so glad to be with Uncle Theo. He said that Uncle Theo is the most interesting man he has ever met. And he's famous, too. When people realize that he is Theodore Frommel, they get very excited and want to know what he is writing about. Martin said that the only soldiers he had seen were Prussian ones.

"In the second letter, Martin described the places that they'd been. He even drew a sketch for me of a beautiful cathedral that he thought I would like. At the end of the letter, he said that they were leaving Toul for Domrémy, the birthplace of Joan of Arc."

"Is that it? Two letters?" Rosemary Rita asked.

"Well, uh, no, I mean yes. Yes, that's all of the letters, but I did get this strange note from him yesterday. He wrote it on one of those new postcards. I have never received one before, have you? Anyway, it didn't make any sense, and it has me worried."

Rosemary Rita's breath caught in her throat. She grabbed Rosemarie's arm. "Where is it? Do you have it with you? Can I see it?"

"I've got it right here in my school bag." Rosemarie took the bag off her arm and placed it on the ground. She rummaged through it for a minute before finding the postcard.

As she held it out, Rosemary Rita sucked in her breath. There it was! She was finally going to learn what the message said.

Chapter 5

THE·MESSAGE·IN
THE·POSTCARD

ROSEMARY RITA STARED AT THE postcard. It was the very same one that she'd read at her own house in Greenville! Only it wasn't 131 years old— here in Berlin, it was just a week old. The card was not bent or yellowed, but crisp and white. She wondered if she'd be able to read the words. Much to her surprise, she had been able to understand German, so maybe she could read the language, too.

As she looked at the fancy script, she realized that it was impossible to figure out. She turned to her great-great-great-grandmother. "Rosemarie, why don't you read Martin's card out loud to me?"

"*Gut.* All right. I'm used to Martin's handwriting. Let's sit over there on the bench," Rosemarie said. As the girls walked to the bench, a flock of pigeons burst into flight, making a terrible racket. The girls got settled, and Rosemarie started to read the message:

> My dear Rosie,
>
> I am sitting here by the statue of Joan of Arc, remembering the magic tricks that our dear uncle used to do. My favorite was when his assistant, dressed in red and blue, would make him disappear. Then you and Aunt Agathe would help find him. Perhaps with a little magic, we will all be together soon.
>
> My love,
>
> Martin

Rosemarie stopped reading and lay the postcard on her lap. A flush came to her cheeks, and she slowly shook her head. "It is such a strange message, I can't figure it out."

"What do you mean? I think it's nice that Martin is remembering old times."

"Well, for one thing, Uncle Theo *never* did magic tricks. And he certainly did not have an assistant dressed in red and blue."

Magic Show:
Cool card tricks
at winslowpress.com

"Are you sure? Maybe you're just forgetting. Martin makes it sound as if your Uncle Theo is just like Houdini."

"Of course I am sure! And who is Houdini?"

"Oops, of course you wouldn't know Houdini. He wasn't even born, I mean, uh, he's not from around here." Rosemary Rita stumbled over her words, trying to cover her mistake.

Rosemarie picked up the postcard and reread it. "I really don't understand this at all. He talks about Aunt Agathe as if she were Uncle Theo's wife. I'm not sure they've even met. I know they haven't been at our apartment at the same time."

"Wait a minute, I just thought of something. What color do the soldiers of the French Army wear?"

"Red and blue, I think. But, Rita, what on earth does that have to do with anything?"

"Well, maybe your brother is sending you a secret message that he didn't want the French soldiers to read. If I am right, I think that your Uncle Theo is in big trouble!" Rosemary Rita exclaimed.

"You think that Martin was trying to tell me that Uncle Theo is in danger? Why?"

"Well, I'm pretty good at decoding messages. My grandmother and I send each other messages in code all the time. When you told me that Uncle Theo never did magic tricks and that he and Aunt Agathe never met, I couldn't help but wonder. Do you think your brother is trying to tell you something?"

Super Sleuth:

Help Rosemary solve another message mystery at winslowpress.com

"No. What I think is that you have a big imagination!"

"Wait! Let's think about this for a minute. Martin talks about a disappearing act. I think that your Uncle Theo has disappeared. Martin mentions the assistant dressed in red and blue. Oh, no! What if that is a code for a soldier from the French army? That would mean your Uncle Theo has been captured!"

"This is awful. You must be wrong!" Rosemarie stood up quickly and started pacing back and forth.

"I wish I was mistaken, but you have to admit it makes sense. There's just one part of the puzzle I can't figure out—Aunt Agathe. Why would Martin include her name? Tell me more about her."

Rosemarie sighed and stood still for a moment. "Aunt Agathe is the most amazing lady I've ever known. Her full name is Agathe Elise Kramer. She is not really my aunt, but a special friend of the family. She never married, probably because she couldn't choose from all of her suitors. I've heard that she was beautiful when she was young. She lives by herself in an apartment a few blocks from my school. Everybody knows her and respects her. She taught for many years at Elisabethschool. Before that she toured Europe with a choral group. She has friends everywhere."

Rosemary Rita jumped up. "Don't you see? That must be why Martin wrote about her in his note. He wants you to go to her for help. We must go see her right away."

"But what if you're wrong about the postcard? And what about school? I am probably late already." Rosemarie grabbed her school bag and started walking away.

"Aunt Agathe can explain later why you didn't get back to school on time," said Rosemary Rita. "This is important. School will have to wait."

Rosemarie stopped and turned around. "Maybe we should go back home and tell Mother and Papa first," she said.

"I don't think just yet. We'll have to tell

them I'm lost, remember? Then they'll want to help me find my parents. But we must do something about Martin's message *now*. Anyway, I bet that Martin sent the postcard to you because he didn't want your parents to worry, especially your mother. You heard what she said at lunch. Your mother is already upset about Martin being in France. This news would be too much for her. Come on, we need to find Aunt Agathe."

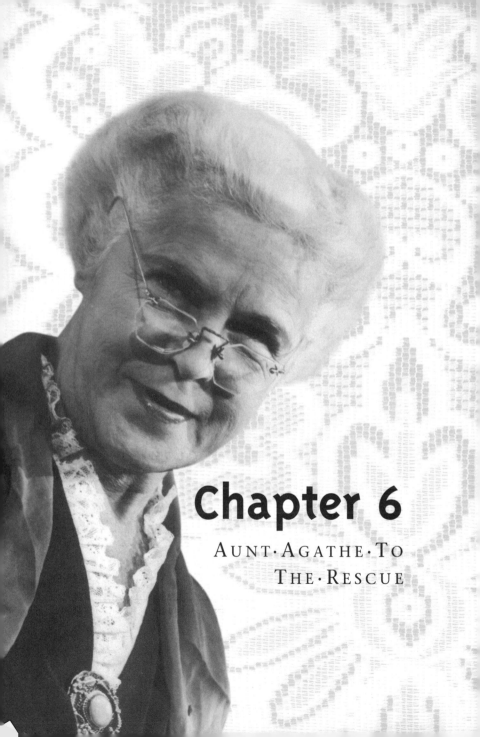

Chapter 6

AUNT·AGATHE·TO THE·RESCUE

ROSEMARIE STUFFED THE POST-card in her school bag and slung it over her shoulder. "Oh, all right," she said. "The quickest way to Aunt Agathe's apartment is to stay on this street. But then we'd pass right by Elisabethschool. I'm afraid someone from school would see me. Let's take the long way around."

Rosemarie grabbed Rosemary Rita's hand and led her across the street. As they walked briskly along, Rosemary Rita dropped back and marveled at all the specialty shops. One

Shopping Spree:

Visit the virtual 1870s store
at winslowpress.com

store had nothing but hats. There were simple felt hats with small brims and fancy hats with birds perched on them. There were also hats with veils and huge, colorful feathers. Rosemary Rita had never seen so many hats!

Another store sold only shoes. The shelves were lined with leather shoes of all sizes. Rosemary Rita caught a glimpse of a cobbler banging on the heel of a black boot. Next to the shoe store was a bakery. Rosemary Rita stopped and smelled the wonderful scent of freshly baked breads. She wished there was time to buy a loaf, but Rosemarie was getting ahead of her. She ran to catch up, making clickety-clack noises on the cobblestones.

"If we go behind the Royal Library, past the University, we will come out onto Leipziger Strauss. Aunt Agathe's apartment is just a few blocks away," Rosemarie said.

Rosemary Rita paused to look at the magnificent royal library building with its huge columns and rows and rows of windows. This trip was longer than she had expected. She wasn't used to walking around in tightly laced boots.

"*Kommen.* Come on," said Rosemarie, pulling her through the enormous courtyard to a gate on the other side. They walked past the university to a very busy street. It reminded Rosemary Rita of New York City, without the cars and taxicabs. There were people scurrying along the sidewalks. Horses pulled elegant carriages across the cobblestones. All of the ladies wore long dresses with their hair piled up on top of their heads—just like Frau Berger's. Some had hats made of felt or wool, and the gentlemen wore coats with vests underneath. Everything was so colorful! It occurred to Rosemary Rita that she had only seen black-and-white photographs of people from the nineteenth century. She had just assumed that people wore nothing but grays and browns. But now she could see vivid blues, greens, and reds.

Finally the two girls turned a corner, and

Rosemarie led them through a gate into a beautiful courtyard. Boxes of flowers rested in front of the windows. The girls walked up to Aunt Agathe's door and knocked. A very small, round lady greeted them. Her gray hair was pulled back in a neat bun shaped like a pincushion. She had on a beautiful loden green dress with brass buttons in a line down the front.

"Rosemarie! What a lovely surprise!" exclaimed Aunt Agathe. She opened her thick arms and wrapped them around Rosemarie in a big hug. "Come in, come in. Please excuse the confusion. I wasn't expecting any visitors. And why aren't you in school? My goodness, who have you brought with you?"

The girls entered the apartment, stepping carefully around the piles of books and objects covering the floor. There did not seem to be an inch of floor or wall space that wasn't covered. The pale blue–patterned wallpaper was nearly hidden underneath all the framed artwork. Ornate gold frames surrounded beautiful oil paintings, and in between the furniture were piles of fabric, books, and papers. Aunt Agathe had the same kind of furniture as Rosemarie's family. Everything was just pushed closer together here in the tiny rooms.

"This is my friend Rita. I apologize for surprising you like this, but we really need to talk to you. It's important—that's why I am missing school," exclaimed Rosemarie.

"Hello, Rita. How nice to meet you. It is always a pleasure to see two such lovely young ladies," said Aunt Agathe. She reached out to shake Rosemary Rita's hand.

"I'm glad to meet you, too, Fräulein Kramer."

"I just finished tidying up after lunch." A clean plate, teacup and saucer were set out on the kitchen table. "How about some nice, refreshing lemonade? I'll get the glasses...."

Rosemarie spoke up quickly. "No, we're fine. I really came to talk to you about Martin and his godfather, Uncle Theo."

Rosemary Rita was a little disappointed. That lemonade sounded delicious, but she did not say anything.

Rosemarie continued, "Aunt Agathe, I just received this strange postcard from Martin. He talks about a magic trick—you know, a disappearing act. We are afraid that Uncle Theo is the one who has disappeared. Well, not disappeared, exactly, but been taken prisoner by the French! Rita was the one who figured it out by the assistant's clothes."

"Wait a minute, dear. You are going too fast. Now, let's start at the beginning. You say you received a card from Martin?"

"Yes, a postcard."

"A postcard, how interesting. I have never seen one. Do you have it with you?"

Rosemary Rita was surprised to hear Aunt

Agathe say she had never seen a postcard. Weren't they invented yet? She would have to do some research when she got back home.

Post It:

Explore the postcard gallery and create your own postcard at winslowpress.com

Rosemarie rustled through her bag for the postcard and handed it to Aunt Agathe. "You see what we mean? Do you think that Rita is right? Do you think that Uncle Theo has been taken prisoner?"

"It is an odd message," said Aunt Agathe as she finished reading it. "However, perhaps Martin is just remembering things incorrectly. Did you notice, he never says Theo's name, just 'our dear uncle.' Maybe he is referring to another uncle. Of course, that wouldn't explain why he says that I helped with the magic trick. I don't know what to make of this."

"Aunt Agathe, don't you think we should do something? If Uncle Theo has been captured, then my brother is all alone in France. And Uncle Theo must have all of the money. How will Martin eat? Where will he stay?"

"You are right, dear. We should at least look into the matter. Hopefully, we will find out it is nothing. Let's take a trip to the Ministry. My nephew, Hans Erdmann, works there. He will know what to do next. Just put your worries aside. Your Aunt Agathe has been in worse trouble than this. Did I ever tell you about the time I was traveling in Salzburg? I got separated from the rest of the choral group. I was a pretty good singer at that time. Of course, now my voice is scruffy, and it sounds awful. Anyway, there I was, seventeen and all alone, away from home, and without a penny to my name. Well, it was the most incredible thing. A very handsome man in a coach offered me a ride back to Berlin. I never should have accepted. I was a foolish girl, however, and I did. He told me his name was Otto. Well, years later, I figured out that he was Otto von Bismarck. Can you imagine? Me, riding in a carriage with the great Otto von Bismarck all the way from Salzburg to Berlin? I have had some adventures in my day, but that may top them all."

"Aunt Agathe, can we please go now?" pleaded Rosemarie.

"Of course, dear, there'll be time for stories later."

Aunt Agathe lifted her hat off the stand and placed it on her head. She wrapped a shawl around her shoulders and picked up an embroidered bag. The girls followed her out of the apartment, closing the door behind them.

Chapter 7

A·CALL·FOR·HELP

AUNT AGATHE, ROSEMARIE, and Rosemary Rita set off at a brisk pace to the Ministry. "Where is Mom with the Suburban when I need her?" thought Rosemary Rita. "My boots are so tight, I'm getting a blister!"

As they hurried along, Rosemary Rita quickly forgot her aching feet. She was too busy trying to see as much as possible of the bustling streets of Berlin. The tops of the gray buildings, with their fancy swirls and curves, looked like icing on a wedding cake. Rosemary Rita marveled at the ornate archways, railings, and columns.

The sidewalks were lined with trees. Two little boys, rolling big hoops to each other, laughed as they avoided hitting pedestrians. The wide streets were dotted with carriages taking passengers where they wanted to go. Vendors with overflowing wagons called out to passersby, urging them to buy their wares.

Before Rosemary Rita knew it, they had arrived at the Ministry. The building was four stories high and had lots of steps leading to two large wooden doors. Aunt Agathe started breathing heavily as they climbed the steps. She paused for a minute as the girls leaped ahead.

"I'm not as spry as I used to be," she panted. "When I was younger, I could climb a mountain in the blink of an eye. Why, I remember that while traveling with my family in Austria in 1817, I climbed..."

"Aunt Agathe! Are you all right?" Rosemarie called from the top of the stairs.

"Of course I am, dear," gasped Aunt Agathe as she slowly mounted the last of the steps.

Once inside the building of the Ministry, Aunt Agathe led the girls to Hans's office. The shoes of the little group clattered on the shiny marble floor. Rosemary Rita noticed that only men were working at the desks. They lifted their eyes as the two young girls and the older lady made their way deliberately through the building.

A clerk with red hair was sitting in front of Hans's office. He stood immediately and said, "We do not usually see children here."

Rosemarie and Rosemary Rita looked at each other. They rolled their eyes at the clerk's comment.

Aunt Agathe spoke right up. "*Guten Tag.* Good afternoon. I am Agathe Kramer. And, as you can see, I am not a child. We came to see Hans Erdmann. Would you be so kind as to tell him we are here?"

"I'm afraid that is impossible. Herr Erdmann is in a meeting right now and cannot be disturbed."

"Oh, no! What are we going to do? We

have to see him. We have a *big* problem!" Rosemary Rita exclaimed.

"Don't worry, dear, I'll take care of this," Aunt Agathe said. She turned to the clerk. "It really is quite urgent that we speak to Hans. We will wait while you tell him that his Aunt Agathe is here."

The clerk hesitated, but Aunt Agathe's steady glare convinced him that he should obey. He went back to tell his boss of their arrival.

He returned quickly and stammered as he spoke. "I apologize, F-F-Fräulein Kramer. Herr Erdmann w-w-will see you. He asks that you just wait a moment as he finishes his meeting."

As they waited, Aunt Agathe told the girls more stories.

"Rosemarie, do you think that Rita would like to hear about the time I fell in the fountain in the center of town?" She did not even pause for a response.

"It was quite hilarious. I was dressed in my fanciest Sunday dress. My father was taking us to throw a coin in the fountain and make a wish. My brother threw his coin in quickly, made his wish, and ran to play on the steps. Next, my sister tossed her coin in, made a wish, and sat on a bench reading a book. It was my turn, but I was taking my time. This was a special event, and I wanted to enjoy every moment of it. Besides, I had to think of the perfect wish.

Make a Wish:

Visit Rosemarie's wishing fountain
at winslowpress.com

"I thought and thought, then finally threw my coin in and made a wish. Well, as soon as I did, I realized it was a terrible mistake. I changed my mind and wanted to make a different one. As I reached into the fountain to get my coin back and start over, my brother shouted at me. He startled me so, I lost my balance and fell headfirst into the water! Oh, I was a sight—dripping wet from head to toe! My father couldn't stop laughing. I was lucky he thought it was funny, as he could have been furious! It was my best dress."

Rosemarie and Rosemary Rita giggled as Aunt Agathe described her father's belly laugh, her voice rising as she got more and more excited. They were still laughing as Hans walked out of his office to greet them.

"Why, Aunt Agathe, what brings you here? And who are these two lovely young ladies you've brought along?" Hans asked.

"My, Hans, it's been too long! How are your dear parents? Last time I saw them, they were about to leave for Bonn. I wish I could have gone with them. I so enjoy it there. Did I ever tell you about the time . . ."

Rosemarie whispered to Rosemary Rita, "Here we go again!"

" . . . we were all traveling together? Our carriage collided with another one that had come out of nowhere. My goodness, it was terrible. Oh dear, listen to me go on and on. It is wonderful to see you, but I'm afraid we are here on serious business. This is Rosemarie Berger, Wilhelm's daughter, and her friend Rita Hampton," Aunt Agathe explained to her nephew.

"Nice to meet both of you. Perhaps we would be more comfortable in my office. It is right this way." Hans adjusted his glasses and led them into his office. They sat down, and Rosemarie pulled out the postcard from Martin. She handed it to Hans.

"Herr Erdmann, I just received this postcard from my brother Martin. He is traveling in France with his godfather, the author Theo Frommel. Uncle Theo is writing a book about the Franco-Prussian War. Martin learned to speak French in school, so Uncle Theo invited him along to be his companion. I received two letters from him and then this...."

"We think Martin wrote a coded message to tell of Uncle Theo being captured by a French soldier," Rosemary Rita interrupted.

Rosemarie shot a quick glance at Rosemary Rita. Then she continued the story, "You see, the message on the card makes no sense. Martin writes about a disappearing act involving Uncle Theo and an assistant dressed in red and blue...."

"Exactly the colors of the uniforms worn by the French soldiers. I figured out that Martin must have been trying to tell us that a French soldier had taken Uncle Theo prisoner," Rosemary Rita blurted.

"I was going to tell him that, Rita!" said Rosemarie.

"Now girls, let's remember—we are all trying to help," said Aunt Agathe.

Hans took off his glasses and laid them on his desk. He rubbed his fingers along the side of his face. Finally he spoke. "Hmm. I'm not sure that this is related, but we have received word that prisoners were taken in Domrémy."

"That proves it!"

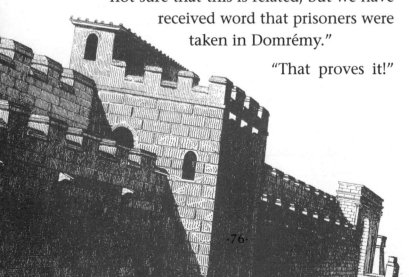

exclaimed Rosemary Rita.

"Well, we can't be certain, but it is a strong possibility. You girls were very clever to figure out the message from Martin. I promise to look into the matter immediately. Now that we have the name Theo Frommel, we will get much further. I will notify you as soon as I have news."

"*Danke schön.* Thank you, Herr Erdmann!" said Rosemarie. "I hope to hear from you soon." The three opened the door, nearly knocking over the clerk. They walked down the hallway and out of the building.

Rosemary Rita smiled. "Well, we've done what we could for your Uncle Theo."

Rosemarie agreed. "Yes, but I am still worried. I wish there was more that we could do."

Aunt Agathe placed her arm around Rosemarie's shoulder. "I have faith in Hans. He will do everything possible to free Uncle Theo. I am proud of you and Rita for all that you did. That was not an easy message to figure out! Now, my stomach is growling. How about a bite to eat?"

"That would be great. Thanks for your help, Aunt Agathe. I have just one more favor to ask. Would you write a note to Fräulein Schmidt at school and explain why I missed the afternoon session?"

"I'd be happy to." Aunt Agathe gave each of the girls an apple from her bag. Then she reached in for some paper and a pen. She quickly wrote the note and handed it to Rosemarie.

"Good-bye, Aunt Agathe. Thank you again," said Rosemarie.

"I enjoyed meeting you, Fräulein Kramer," added Rosemary Rita.

"*Auf Wiedersehen.* Good-bye. Hurry home, girls," called Aunt Agathe.

Chapter 8

HOME·AGAIN

THE GIRLS SKIPPED ALONG THE road to the Berger's apartment. They munched their apples and watched the people pass by. They didn't talk much, as they were both thinking about Martin.

Rosemarie led Rosemary Rita up the back outside stairs to the kitchen. She hung her school bag on the hook by the china cabinet. The two girls slipped off their cloaks.

"Hello, Rosemarie," said Frau Berger as she wiped Fritz's hands and face with a towel. He wiggled loose to see his big sister. "You are just in time to help me peel the potatoes for supper. Hello, Rita. It is nice to see you again, but shouldn't you be getting home?"

Rosemarie quickly spoke up. "Mother, we didn't get a chance to tell you before, with all of the excitement about Papa and the carriage for the prince. Rita can't find her parents. She lost them while they were traveling through Berlin."

"Oh my! I wish you had told me earlier. Rita, dear, your parents must be worried sick about you. We must do something right away. When Meister Berger comes up from the workshop, I will ask him what he thinks."

Fritz planted himself in Rosemarie's lap. As Rosemary Rita watched him, she felt a tiny pang for Ryan.

Frau Berger took Fritz from Rosemarie so the girls could start peeling potatoes. Rosemary Rita struggled with the little knife to get the skin off. Rosemarie, on the other hand, was an expert. She peeled five potatoes in the time it took Rosemary Rita to finish one.

As the girls worked, Rosemary Rita heard

feet pounding up the steps. There was a rustling at the door as Meister Berger and his apprentice Karl entered the kitchen.

Frau Berger dashed over to her husband and helped him out of his work apron. "Wilhelm, Rosemarie's friend is lost," she said. "She cannot find her parents. What should we do?"

Wilhelm Berger turned to Rita. "Where were you when you were separated?"

Rosemary Rita panicked as she tried to think of an answer. "Not far from here," she finally blurted. "Rosemarie knows the spot, because she found me right after I lost them."

"It was just around the corner on Leipziger Strauss," explained Rosemarie.

Meister Berger tugged on his moustache. "We should leave word at the Ministry that we have found her. Unfortunately, it is closed for the evening."

Rosemarie and Rosemary Rita gave each other a knowing look. They had just been there!

He continued, "Rita, you can stay here for

the night. First thing in the morning, we will work on finding your parents."

"Thank you, Meister Berger!" exclaimed Rosemary Rita.

Beyond Schnitzel!:

German food and recipes
at winslowpress.com

At supper they ate slices of boiled potatoes with an egg and some dry bread. Everyone drank coffee, even the children. Rosemary Rita took one sip and spit it out. She hoped that no one noticed.

After dinner, Meister Berger gathered everyone in the living room. He sat in the big green velvet winged chair. Frau Berger sat on the settee with Fritz close beside her. Rosemarie motioned to Rosemary Rita to join her on the hooked rug in front of her father. Meister Berger lifted a heavy blue book and turned to the marked page.

Before he started reading, he explained to Rosemary Rita, "Tonight I am going to read *Kannitverstan* by Johann Peter Hebel."

He cleared his throat and began reading:

A German journeyman is traveling through Amsterdam. He sees an especially beautiful large house with six chimneys and fine cornices and high windows. The garden is full of tulips and other flowers. When he asks the name of the man who owns the fine home, he is told, "Kannitverstan."

These are three Dutch words (though the journeyman heard them as one word) that mean "I cannot understand you." The journeyman, however, thought them to be the name of the lucky rich homeowner.

After a while, he arrives in the harbor and sees many ships. He notices one in particular that has just been unloaded. The journeyman marvels at the many crates full of sugar, coffee, rice, and paper. Curious, he stops one of the men carrying a crate off the ship. "What is the name of the fortunate man who owns the ship?" he asks. "To whom do all of these riches belong?"

Again, the answer is "Kannitverstan."

"Why, it's the same man who built the magnificent house," thinks the journeyman. "I am poor compared to this rich man."

Soon thereafter, the journeyman meets a large funeral procession. Many mourners are following a black-covered hearse, drawn by four black horses.

He tells one of the mourners, "This must have been a good friend of yours that makes you follow his coffin so full of sorrow."

"Kannitverstan" is the answer.

The journeyman feels both sad and relieved as he walks with the funeral procession. He thinks about poor Kannitverstan and how in the end every man, rich or poor, ends up the same. He leaves with a light heart. After that, when he thought about the rich people in the world and how he was so poor by comparison, he remembered Mr. Kannitverstan in Amsterdam. This made him feel better.

Meister Berger closed the book and placed it back on the table. Gabi Berger stood to kiss her daughter. "Time for bed, girls. Rosemarie, take the pillow and blanket from Martin's room for Rita. Sleep well."

Silly Stories:

Create a ridiculous story about yourself and your friends at winslowpress.com

As they settled into bed, Rosemarie said, "I'm so tired. What a day!"

Rosemary Rita yawned. "What a day is right!" She pulled the itchy wool blanket over herself. The two girls were both asleep in no time.

Chapter 9

LONGING·FOR·HOME

EARLY THE NEXT MORNING, a messenger knocked at the door of the Berger home. Frau Berger answered the door. A young man with blond hair and a moustache, dressed in a Prussian uniform, stood in the doorway. He was carrying a small brown parcel in his hand.

"Frau Berger?" he asked.

"*Ja*. Yes."

"My name is Georg Reinhardt. I have just returned from France, where I met your son Martin...."

Frau Berger let out a gasp and nearly fainted. "Is Martin all right?" she asked.

"Please don't worry, he is fine. He asked me to give this package to his sister and to send word that he would be returning home soon," the soldier said.

Frau Berger took the package and placed it on the small table by the door. Then she turned to Georg. "Thank you, thank you, you are so kind to go out of your way. Tell me, where did you see Martin and how did he look?"

"I met him in Toul. He looked fine. He said that he was headed to Domrémy with his uncle. After that they will be coming home."

"I'm so glad! That is wonderful. Oh, forgive my manners. Won't you please come in and join us for breakfast?"

"I appreciate your kind offer, but I must be on my way. Good-bye."

Frau Berger shook Georg's hand and waved after him as he walked away. Then she closed the door and ran into the bedroom to tell her husband the good news.

At breakfast, Lina set the table with the blue-and-white china. The family sat down and ate rolls with a plum spread and coffee. This time Rosemary Rita did not try a sip of the coffee.

"You see, Gabi, I told you that Martin was going to be fine. It was a good experience for him to help his uncle and practice his French," remarked Meister Berger.

"I suppose you are right. I do feel better after talking with that nice soldier, Georg."

"I want to see the soldier, Papa," demanded Fritz.

Meister Berger laughed and said, "Next time, son."

Rosemary Rita did not join in the conversation. All of the talk about Martin coming home made her worry about how *she* was going to get back to Greenville. When she'd first arrived, everything had been different and exciting. She had been caught up in the adventure. Now she wondered if she would be stuck here forever. There was a panicky feeling in her chest.

"What if I can't get back to the twenty-first century? And never see Mom or Dad or Mimi or even Ryan again?" she worried.

Rosemary Rita's eyes filled with tears. She knew that in a moment she would no longer be able to hide her worries. Quietly excusing herself, she grabbed her cloak and went out to the courtyard.

She looked at the outhouse and thought about all of the things she missed at home: her room with twin four-poster beds, her books and stuffed animals, her bathroom, computer and rollerblades, the television and telephone. She thought about cars, planes, and motorboats. She thought about Skittles and Gatorade and all of her favorite foods. But more than anything, she thought about her family.

Fabulous Favorites:

Compare favorites with Rosemary Rita at winslowpress.com

She pictured her mom combing her hair and making her pancakes with the syrup in a little cup on the side. She remembered snuggling up with her dad to watch golf on

TV and the way they listened to music together as he drove her to school. She thought about Ryan and how he would scream her name—"Row-may-we-wheat-uh"—when he saw her. She could almost feel his tiny hands wrapped around her legs. And of course, she thought of Mimi and the postcards.

"I can't live here forever, I just can't!"

The tears began flowing down her face.

"If I ever get home again, I promise to never take things for granted. I am going to be the best big sister and daughter in the world!" Rosemary Rita said out loud.

Just then, Rosemarie came out into the courtyard. "Rita, are you all right?"

Rosemary Rita wiped the tears from her face. "I'm fine," she lied. "I guess all of the talk about Martin coming home made me miss my home and family."

"Oh, my goodness. I have been so terrible. In my excitement, I forgot all about you getting separated from your parents. Come inside; let's remind Papa of his plan to help you."

"Rosemarie, I don't think your father or anyone else can help me. I don't know what I'm going to do."

"Now, don't be silly. Of course we can do something. If it weren't for you, I might never have figured out the message on the postcard. Hans just sent word that volunteers from the government and church as well as private citizens are working to secure Uncle Theo's release. He feels certain that they will have him out in no time. You see, it truly is a day for celebration. Now come with me. Mama just remembered that the soldier brought a package for me from Martin. Let's go open it."

Rosemary Rita followed Rosemarie into the house. Rosemarie picked up the package from the small table and led Rosemary Rita to her room.

"I love presents," said Rosemarie. "What

do you think could be inside? I wonder if it's art supplies. Martin promised he would try to find some for me. Or maybe it is a new doll. I am sure that a doll from France would be absolutely beautiful."

"Hurry up and open it! Then you'll *know* what's inside!"

"I know, I know. I just think half the fun of a present is wondering what it could be. But you're right. I'll open it."

Rosemarie pulled off the string and ripped the brown paper from the package. There was a bundle of white cloth. She carefully unwrapped the cloth to reveal an hourglass. *The* hourglass!

Rosemary Rita blurted, "That's it, that's the hourglass! Oh, I can't believe it."

"What do you mean, 'that's the hourglass'?"

"It's the one that—" Rosemary Rita stopped in midsentence. Of course, she could never explain the hourglass. Rosemarie would think she was nuts. "I just meant that I love hourglasses. I love to watch the sand fall from one part to the other."

"Oh, me, too. Isn't Martin the best brother there ever was? He took the time to find something special for me. I'm going to keep this hourglass forever."

Rosemary Rita sighed with relief. This was definitely the same hourglass she had flipped over in her bedroom. It had the same wooden stand with ancient writing carved on it and the picture of the man with the boat on the water. She had never seen anything quite like it.

Rosemary Rita thought, "I wonder why nothing happened to Martin when he touched it. I'll have so much to ask Mimi when I get home. And I know I will be home soon. If only I could be alone with the hourglass."

Just then, Frau Berger called, "Rosemarie, please come here. I need your help in the kitchen."

"All right, Mother. I'm coming." Rosemarie

carefully lay the
hourglass on her bed. "I'll be right
back, Rita."

"Good-bye, Rosemarie," said Rosemary
Rita as she hugged her great-great-great-
grandmother.

Rosemarie laughed. "I'll be right back,
silly," she said. Then she left the room.

"I know, but hopefully, *I* won't be here,"
thought Rosemary Rita. "I'll never forget our
wonderful time together." She looked at the

hourglass, almost afraid to try it in case it didn't work. She hesitated for a moment and thought about leaving a note. But since she didn't know how long Rosemarie would be out of the room, she had to move quickly. Besides, Rosemarie couldn't read English, so it wouldn't do any good to write her a good-bye message.

As Rosemary Rita hurried over to the hourglass, she tripped on the laces from Frau Berger's boots. She looked down at her feet. "Oops, I almost forgot." She undid the laces and yanked the boots off. Then she picked up the hourglass and turned it over. Holding her breath, she dropped it on the bed and fell back into the pillows.

As the sand in the hourglass began to drip down to the bottom, the feeling came over her again. She felt funny, kind of light in the head. Her stomach felt queasy, as if she'd just stepped off a roller-coaster ride. Suddenly, everything became blurry and she slipped off into a deep, deep sleep.

Timing Is Everything:

Crazy time-travel ideas and inventions at winslowpress.com

Chapter 10
A · VISIT · WITH · MIMI

WHEN ROSEMARY RITA awoke, she reached around and felt her pillow. She knew before she even opened her eyes that she was back in her room again. Rolling over, she glanced at the clock by her bed. It read 2:33 P.M. Only one hour had passed. Was everything that had happened just a dream?

Rosemary Rita scampered over to the mirror that hung on the door and looked at herself. She was still wearing the dress and pinafore. "Well, I guess this outfit can go back in the box," she said.

"Where are my jeans?" She undid the

Time Check:

Find out what time it is anywhere in the world at winslowpress.com

buttons on the dress and lifted it over her head. Her jeans and long-sleeved T-shirt were still in a pile on the floor. She got dressed and raced downstairs to find her mother. Mom was sitting in the playroom with Ryan in her lap, trying to tie his shoes. Rosemary Rita gave them both a big hug.

"I love you, Mom! I love you, Ryan!"

"We love you, too, sweetie. Thanks." Her mother looked up, bewildered.

Rosemary Rita gazed at the purple dinosaur that Ryan was watching on TV. "Boy, I never thought I'd be so happy to see that show again. But I am." She twirled around, touching the familiar objects on the mantelpiece—the blue Wedgewood tea set, the brass candlesticks, and the framed picture of her and Ryan. Then she raced from room to room, noticing all the familiar things that she had missed.

"I need to call Mimi!" she said as she

came full circle back to the stairs. "And I need to call her *now!*"

Rosemary Rita bounded upstairs to her parents' room and dialed her grandmother's number. While the phone was ringing, she thought about what she was going to say. Now she understood why Mimi had told her to wait before opening the shiny red package with the hourglass inside.

"Of course," mused Rosemary Rita, "she knows me so well, she should have guessed that I would be too curious to wait."

The phone kept ringing until finally she heard her grandmother's voice. "I cannot come to the phone right now, but if you'll kindly leave a message, I'll get back to you as soon as possible." *Beep.*

"Hi, Mimi. It's me, Rosemary Rita. Thanks for the packages. They were the best birthday gifts ever. But I really need to talk to you. Right away! Call me. Love you. Bye."

Just then she heard her mother yelling, "*Rosemary Rita!*"

"Okay, coming."

Rosemary Rita ran to the top of the steps. She looked down and couldn't believe her eyes. There was Mimi standing next to her mother!

"Mimi. Oh, Mimi, you're here. I'm so glad to see you." Rosemary Rita raced down the stairs and threw herself into her grandmother's arms. As she snuggled close to her, she smelled the familiar scent of lilac from Mimi's bubble bath. "I've been dying to talk to you. I didn't know you were coming."

"Well, dear, what a wonderful greeting. You always make me feel so good. I hadn't planned on coming, but I decided that I needed to talk to you in person about your birthday gift. You see, I sent you ten packages...."

"I know, we picked them up already. I've opened some of them, and I was just trying to phone you when Mom called."

Mimi sighed. "I hoped I would arrive before the boxes did."

"Mimi, do you want to come to my room so we can look at them together?"

"That would be great." She turned to her daughter. "Is that okay with you?"

"Sure. I'm going to take Ryan outside to play for a bit. You two have fun! I can't wait to see what's in those boxes! I'll come see them later." Mom picked up Ryan and took him out to the backyard.

Rosemary Rita stared at her grandmother. Her auburn hair was cut to just above her chin. Her tortoiseshell glasses magnified her big blue eyes. Today she had on navy blue linen slacks with a white short-sleeved sweater and a cardigan tied over her shoulders. Her gold charm bracelet jingled as they walked up the stairs and down the hall to Rosemary Rita's room.

Mimi looked at the pile of postcards on the bed, then at the open boxes. Finally she noticed the shiny red paper on the floor and the hourglass on the bed.

"Oh, Rosemary, you opened it! I asked you not to. That's really why I came down. I started thinking that I should have given you these boxes in person. I really thought that I would beat the boxes here. You see, honey, this hourglass is very special...."

Chapter 11

THE·BROKEN·LOCKET

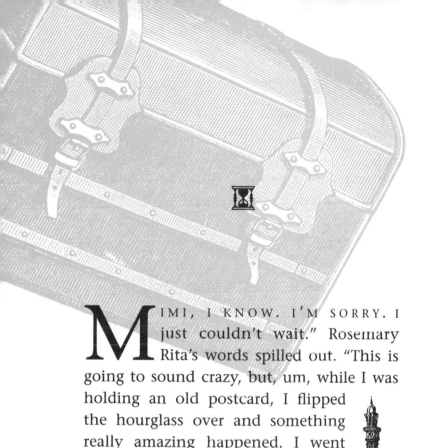

MIMI, I KNOW. I'M SORRY. I just couldn't wait." Rosemary Rita's words spilled out. "This is going to sound crazy, but, um, while I was holding an old postcard, I flipped the hourglass over and something really amazing happened. I went back in time! Back a hundred and thirty-one years. I met Rosemarie Ruth Berger, the first Rosemary. She was just ten years old, like me. Oh, it was great. We had a real adventure." Rosemary Rita told her grandmother every detail of her trip, her voice rising with excitement.

"So it worked!" Mimi listened carefully, then got a faraway look in her eyes. Finally she said, "As the years passed, I often wondered whether my adventure with the hourglass had been just a dream. But I see that you really did go back in time. You couldn't have dreamed all of those details. Did you know that the Uncle Theo you helped rescue wrote a famous book called *Prisoner of France*? I read it in college and found out that he was rescued, but it took a couple of months to get him out of France. It really is fascinating, isn't it?"

"Oh, yes!" cried Rosemary Rita. "And I am so relieved to find out that Uncle Theo made it home safely. Do you think that Rosemarie and I helped get him out?"

"Of course I do. Aunt Agathe deserves credit, too. She sounds like a character."

"You would have liked her, Mimi. She was so funny, always telling us stories. And she was so little. She came up to about here on me." Rosemary Rita pointed to her chest.

Mimi took her hand. "Now sit down and

I will tell you everything I know about the hourglass and the postcards.

"When I was ten years old, just like you, I was playing in my grandmother's attic. I loved to play up there. She had so much stuff, I found something different every time I went up to the attic to explore. Well, one time I found an old trunk that was covered with dust. I opened it up and found all of the same things that I just sent to you. I looked through the postcards and the treasures and got particularly interested in a postcard from Paris written in 1889. As I held it up to look at the picture, I flipped the hourglass over. Then, *whoosh*, I went back in time, just as you did."

Rosemary Rita let out a squeal, "Wow! This is so cool. Hey, what about Mom? Did she ever go back in time?"

"No, she never had a chance. I tried one more time, when I was eleven, but nothing happened. My mother stored the trunk in a closet after my grandmother moved. I didn't discover it again until last year, when Mother died and I was cleaning out her house so I could sell it. That's why your mother never experienced the magic. When she was ten, the trunk was shut up in a dark closet."

"Maybe we can all go back in time together," Rosemary Rita suggested.

"I don't believe that would work, sweetie. As I said, it only worked for me when I was ten. I think that is part of the magic."

"Well, that would explain why nothing happened to Martin when *he* touched the hourglass."

"Yes...." Mimi got that faraway look in her eyes again. Then she sighed and said, "All my life, I've wanted to go back. It was so incredible. I went to the Paris Exposition, the World's Fair in 1889. There were people there from all over the world. The ladies and gentlemen wore very fashionable clothing and strolled up and down the paths. I will never forget the sights as long as I live. I didn't stay long, though, because by accident I flipped the hourglass over and was back home in a jiffy."

"So the key is to hold the hourglass in your hand? Then you can come back whenever you want to?"

"Yes. And the post-card is important, too. It determines where you go."

"I was lucky Martin sent the hourglass when he did. Otherwise I might have been trapped in the past forever!" said Rosemary Rita.

Mimi leaned over and kissed her granddaughter. "Oh, darling, your adventure sounds like it was a little risky. I am so glad that nothing happened to you."

"I'm okay, really I am. Oh, but Mimi, I just thought of something. When I went back in time, do you think that my presence changed the future?"

"That's an interesting point. I suppose we

will never know. Perhaps it's all part of the magic."

"Well, now that I know about the magic and how it works, could I take another trip back in time? Oh, please, could I?" Rosemary Rita begged.

"Now, slow down. Don't you think you've had enough adventure for one day? Why don't we look through these postcards? You can decide where you might like to go next. This time we can do some planning so that you are better prepared."

They sat together and looked through the postcards. Mimi found the one from the Paris Exposition.

"Oh, look, there it is. The postcard that took me to Paris! I can't believe it! This picture really doesn't do it justice. It was much more beautiful. This doesn't show all the magnificent colors."

"You know, I wondered about the history of postcards when Aunt Agathe said that she had never seen one."

"Yes, they were a new invention when you

were in Germany. Probably postcards had only been available for a few months when Rosemarie received hers from her brother. During the Franco-Prussian War, hot-air balloons carried postcards out of France."

"Cool. Was this postcard from Paris made before there were color postcards?" asked Rosemary Rita.

"Yes, color postcards were still a few years away. Let me read you the message. That's what fascinated me." Mimi translated the words from French to English as she read.

June 12th, 1889

Dear Gracie,

I can't believe we are going to meet face to face. Did you get my package? Please wear the locket so I'll know it's you.

Before she got to the second paragraph, Rosemary Rita jumped up and started rustling through Box #3. Underneath the old newspaper was the object she was searching for. She grabbed it and said, "Mimi, do you think this is the locket they were talking about?"

"Could be, dear. Now, why don't we put all this away for a while? Let's go downstairs and get a bite to eat."

"Okay, but only if you promise that before you leave, you will help me go on another trip back in time. I'd like to see the Paris Exposition and find out what happened with the locket. Half of it seems to be missing."

"I never did find out why. I think it would be wonderful if you could find out more about it. We'll plan the whole trip ahead of time, but not today. Okay? One adventure per day is enough!"

Talk Back!:

Send a message to Rosemary Rita
at winslowpress.com

They both laughed. Rosemary Rita reached for her grandmother's warm hand. She held it as they walked out of the room. Glancing back at the broken locket she had left on her bed, she began to think of their wonderful secret and where it would lead her next.

About the Author

*I have wished many times over the years that my
children could have known my grandmother, Mimi.
I am thrilled that her spirit comes to life in these books.
Now I can share Mimi with my own children and
many other children as well.*

—**BARBARA ROBERTSON**

Barbara Robertson lives in Greenville, South Carolina, with her
husband, Marsh, and their three children, Ashley, Will, and
Eileen. She has earned B.A. and M.A. degrees in Elementary and
Early Childhood Education. A former teacher, Barbara enjoys vol-
unteering at her children's schools. In addition, she serves on
several community boards (Children's Hospital, Friends of the
Greenville Zoo, and the South Carolina Children's Theatre). When
she's not pounding on her word processor or chauffeuring her
children, you might find Barbara on the tennis court or curled up
with a good book.   *Photo: Kay Roper*

A Note from the Author

At the time of Rosemary Rita's adventure in Berlin, the country of Germany as we know it today did not exist. The German people shared a language and culture, but they lived in many different "states," or kingdoms. Each of these states had its own government and its own royal family. Two of the largest states were Austria and Prussia.

By 1870, when Rosemarie Ruth Berger was ten years old, most of the northern states, except for Austria, had joined together in the North German Alliance. Prussia was the leader of the alliance, and Rosemarie's hometown of Berlin was the capital city of Prussia. She was living in an important city at an important time. During the autumn of 1870, the Chancellor of Prussia, Otto von Bismarck, was trying to join the North German Alliance with the southern German states. If he succeeded, he would become the ruler of a large country.

At the same time, the Franco-Prussian War was being fought. France and Prussia had disagreed about who the next king of Spain should be. For several years, the Spanish throne had been empty, and it looked as though a south German prince, a relative of Prussia's King Wilhelm I, would become king. The French felt that this would give Prussia too much power over Europe. If Prussia were to control the German states *and* the country of Spain, it would become the most powerful country in Europe.

In our story, the Bergers allowed their son Martin to visit France during the war. Even so, they were worried about him. Although he was with his Uncle Theo and was expected to keep clear of any fighting, he was still behind enemy lines. Martin's parents placed a great deal of trust in Uncle Theo, who was an experienced traveler.

The character of Uncle Theo is based on a real person, a writer named Theodor Fontane. Fontane wrote about the war for a Berlin newspaper, the *Kreuzzeitung*, during the Franco-Prussian War. He was also a travel writer and novelist. He is remembered today in Germany as one of the country's most important writers. There are even schools named after him.

When Martin Berger shared secret information with his family while in France, he wrote it in code. Code was necessary because the French authorities read mail that was going to Prussia. This was especially easy to do with a message written on a postcard like the one Martin sent to his sister Rosemarie.

At the time of the Franco-Prussian War, postcards were a fairly new invention. During the 1860s, European businesses began to send much of their correspondence (such as invoices or announcements) on single cards, rather than using paper and envelopes. These cards were a way of saving both paper and money on postage. An Austrian professor noticed that much of the correspondence sent by the public in the form of letters could just as well be sent on cards that would take up less space and also be cheaper. On October 1, 1869, the world's first postcard was produced by the Austrian Postal Administration.

The cards became popular immediately, and millions were sold. Other countries followed Austria's lead, and suddenly the cards were not just a paper-saving device. Featuring scenes of historic buildings or cities or even poems and advertisements, postcards were a hot new trend. Rosemarie Berger would have been thrilled to have gotten one of these cards, and not just because it came from her brother. Most children her age would not have received much, if any, mail, and a trendy postcard would have been especially exciting!

Life for a girl of Rosemarie Berger's age meant lots of school. In Prussia, eight years of school were required by law. Starting at age six, Prussian children attended school Monday through Saturday every week.

Saturdays were half days, and there was a six-week summer vacation. The Elisabethschool in Berlin, which Rosemarie attended, was a well-known girls' school founded in 1747.

Rosemarie and her classmates at the Elisabethschool would have studied many of the same subjects taught to students today, such as reading, math, history, and geography. Probably they were also taught other things that were considered necessary at the time. Girls studied "handiwork" (needlework and crafts) and calligraphy (lettering). Before Christmas or other holidays, teachers would help them make gifts for their families. Rosemarie's class would also have started learning French that year (English lessons began earlier).

Most students had two hours a day for lunch and usually went home for a break. Rosemarie's mother spent the morning planning and making lunch, which was the main meal of the day. Good-sized servings of soup, potatoes, meat, and vegetables were an average lunch for a family like Rosemarie's. The children would drink milk (or buttermilk) or perhaps lemonade. At some meals they drank coffee along with the adults, though children's coffee was sometimes diluted with water or extra milk. Frau Berger was cooking for a big group of people, including her husband's apprentices and even some of his other assistants. Although she had a maid to help her, getting lunch together was a big chore.

Running a household with so many people in it was a full-time job. There were washing days, ironing days, and market days to keep track of. Older girls were expected to help with the younger children and also with chores like cooking, cleaning, and ironing. Rosemarie had time to do her schoolwork, but much was expected of her at home as well.

In 1870, children would play outside, rolling hoops down the street or in the courtyard behind the house if the landlord allowed it. Rosemarie and her friends also played with many of the same kinds of toys that children play with today: balls, jump ropes, dolls, toy soldiers, and toy animals. Games like marbles and chess were popular.

Rosemarie's father had a workshop very close to the Berger home—he could reach it by walking through the courtyard of their building. He worked on his coaches for most of the day and kept his business accounts at night. At least one of his apprentices always lived with the family, making the household even bigger. In the evenings, if Herr Berger wasn't working, he might read to the family from a novel or a book of stories, like the tales of the Brothers Grimm. Fritz might have played quietly while Rosemarie helped her mother with sewing or knitting.

On Sundays after church, German families were known to take a stroll through the Tiergarten, Berlin's huge public park. There was a zoo as well as public baths where children could play in the water. In the winter, the children had snowball fights and went ice skating. Neighbors were often invited over for cake and coffee on a Sunday evening. Prussians were well known for their delicious cakes and pastries, full of chocolate and cream. Had our story shown Martin and Uncle Theo returning safely from France, there would have been a big party at the Berger home. All kinds of wonderful treats baked by Frau Berger and Lina and Rosemarie would have been served.

The war went badly for France—and very well for the German states. In November of 1870, a month after Rosemary Rita traveled to Berlin, Germany became a country. The King of Prussia, Wilhelm I, became the emperor (or kaiser) of Germany. The Franco-Prussian War had brought the German states together in support of Prussia, helping Otto von Bismarck achieve his goal of uniting them to form a single country.

German Expressions Used in This Book

Wie heissen Sie? What is your name?
Vee hei'sen zee?

Wohin gehen Sie? Where are you going?
Voh-hin' geh'-en zee?

Wohnung apartment
vohn'-oong

Dies ist meine Freundin. This is my friend.
Dees ist mi'-ne froyn'-din.

Sehr erfreut. Pleased to meet you.
Zehr ehr-froyt.

gut all right
goot

kommen come
kom'-en

Guten Tag. Good afternoon.
Goot'-en tahkh.

Danke schön. Thank you.
Danke shon.

Auf Wiedersehen! Good-bye.
Owf veed'-er-zeh-en!

ja yes
yah

Other Useful Expressions

Wie geht es Ihnen? How are you?
Vee geht es ee'-nen?

Verzeihen Sie mir. Pardon me.
Fer-tsi-en zee meer.

Sprechen Sie Englisch? Do you speak English?
Shpreç'-en zee ehng'-leesh?

Wohin gehen Sie? Where are you going?
Voh-hin' geh'-en zee?

Ich möchte. . . I would like. . .
Iç moeç'-te

Generations

Rosemary Ruth "Rosemarie" Berger (Christianson)
Great-great-great-grandmother

Rosemary Grace "Gracie" Christianson (Gibson)
Great-great-grandmother

Rosemary Anna Gibson (Ryan)
Great-grandmother

Rosemary Regina "Mimi" Ryan (Carlisle)
Grandmother

Rosemary "Leigh" Carlisle (Hampton)
Mother

Rosemary Rita Hampton

of **Rosemarys**

BORN	AGE 10
1860	1870
1879	1889
1909	1919
1935	1945
1965	1975
1991	2001

WHAT'S NEXT?

Read a chapter from Rosemary Rita's next adventure at winslowpress.com